Farewell,
My Lunchbag

Chet Gecko Mysteries

Farewell, My Lunchbag

FROM THE TATTERED CASEBOOK OF

CHET GECKO
PRIVATE EYE

Bruce Hale

HARCOURT, INC.

San Diego • New York • London

Requests for permission to make copies of any part of the
work should be mailed to the following address:
Permissions Department, Harcourt, Inc.,
6277 Sea Harbor Drive, Orlando, Florida 32887-6777.

www.harcourt.com

Library of Congress Cataloging-in-Publication Data
Hale, Bruce.
Farewell, my lunchbag: from the tattered casebook
of Chet Gecko, private eye/Bruce Hale.—1st ed.
p. cm.
"A Chet Gecko Mystery."
Summary: When fourth-grade private eye Chet Gecko is
called to catch someone who is stealing food from the
school cafeteria, he finds himself framed for the crime.
[1. Geckos—Fiction. 2. Animals—Fiction.
3. School lunchrooms, cafeterias, etc.—Fiction.
4. Schools—Fiction. 5. Mystery and detective stories.
6. Humorous stories.] I. Title.
PZ7.H1295Far 2001
[Fic]—dc21 00-8596
ISBN 0-15-202275-9

Text set in Bembo
Display type set in Elroy
Designed by Ivan Holmes

E G H F D

Printed in the United States of America

For all the teachers—from Miss Porter to
Mr. Nash and beyond—who fanned my creative
flame. *Mahalo mucho.*

A private message from the private eye . . .

I've always loved a good mystery. Like, why is the alphabet in that order—is it because of the song? Does geometry actually have a use in the real world? And, what if the Hokey Pokey really *is* what it's all about?

My hunger for mystery is matched only by my appetite for cockroach casserole, mosquito marshmallow surprise, and other cafeteria favorites.

But one time, my taste for good grub landed me in the soup. I tried to help a cafeteria dame who was no honey bun, but a good egg nonetheless. After an appetizer of confusion followed by a main course of grief and aggravation, this detective was almost ready to throw in the dish towel.

Did I stick it out until the end? Let me put it this way: Chet is one gecko who always gets his goodies.

After all, danger may be my business, but dessert is my delight.

1

Fright of the Iguana

Mrs. Bagoong was a hundred pounds of tough, leathery iguana. Her eyes were like chocolate drops, her cheeks soft as AstroTurf and about the same color. Her thick, powerful body was wrapped in a blue apron that said KISS THE COOK.

Yuck. Nobody in his right mind would try to smooch Mrs. Bagoong.

She ruled the lunchroom as head cafeteria lady. If you wanted extra dessert, you had to go through her.

Few tried.

But I've always loved a challenge.

Mrs. Bagoong was all right. For an iguana. So when I saw her frown at lunchtime that day, I was worried.

"What's the story, brown eyes?" I said. "If your face were any longer, you'd have to rent an extra chin."

Mrs. Bagoong piled lime Jell-O onto my tray. The green gelatin was packed with juicy dung beetles. *Yum.* My mouth watered like an automatic sprinkler system.

The queen of the lunchroom sighed. It sounded like a small hurricane. "Chet, honey," said Mrs. Bagoong, "we've got problems."

My heart raced. "You're not running out of mothloaf, are you?"

"Not yet."

I relaxed. "So it's not serious, then."

"Serious enough!" she said. "Someone's stealing our food. If it keeps up, it could put me out of business."

My fists clenched. Food thieves! Scum like that are lower than kidnappers, blackmailers, and people who don't return library books. They stink like leftovers from a hyena's lunchbox.

A plastic tray bumped mine.

"Hubba-hubba, Chet," said Tony Newt. "Sweet-talking the cafeteria ladies, eh?" He winked at me with a bulging eye, one scaly dude to another.

This wasn't the best time for a chat, so I leaned toward Mrs. Bagoong and whispered, "Let's talk after lunch."

"Ooh, lovers' secrets," cooed Tony.

I turned to my classmate. "Hey, Tony, do you know the difference between you and a bug-eating moron?"

His forehead wrinkled. "No, what?"

"Beats me."

Sometimes, I just kill me.

I took my tray and found a seat. While I munched on mothloaf in gravy, I chewed over Mrs. Bagoong's problem.

Food thieves at Emerson Hicky, eh? If they kept up their dirty work, the thieves might put the cafeteria out of commission. And that would derail my Jell-O train.

I had to help Mrs. Bagoong. A dame in distress gets me every time—even when she's a hundred-pound iguana.

Lunch finished, I dropped my tray on the dirty stack and waited for the place to clear out. The line of kids dribbled out the doors like snot from a runny nose in flu season, and the cafeteria workers started cleaning up. (The cafeteria, I mean, not the nose.)

The queen of the lunchroom crooked one claw at me.

"Come here, Chet," said Mrs. Bagoong.

We walked behind the counter, she opened the storeroom door, and I went rubber legged in amazement. Food, food, and more food!

The huge refrigerator sang a siren song louder than a fat lady in a French opera. I plunged my head inside and almost fell down in delight. Pickled spider-eggs and pudding and rat cheese and deep-fried termites and cockroach quiche and happy-spider lasagna and candied butterflies and fire ants in red sauce and—

"Uh, Chet? Anybody home?" said Mrs. Bagoong. She rapped on the door with a thick fist.

"Oh. Sorry." I slowly pulled my head out of gecko heaven and took a deep breath.

"Let's get down to business," I said. "You've got a low-down food thief, and I'm just the gecko to find out who he is."

"Or she," said Mrs. Bagoong.

"Who he or she is."

"Or it."

"Who he, she, or it is." I sighed. "Did you used to be a teacher?"

"For five years," she said, straightening her hair net. "How did you know?"

"Lucky guess. Now tell me all about the food-napping. How did it start?"

Mrs. Bagoong parked her massive bulk on a tub of lima beans. I shuddered. Even uncooked, those things are dangerous. She stroked her scaly chin.

"I first noticed it last week," she said. "I was making carpenter-ant omelettes, and we ran out of eggs."

"Maybe you forgot to buy enough."

"That's what I thought. But then the next day, our candied butterflies disappeared. And two days after that, some bananas went missing."

I held up a hand.

"Let me get this straight," I said. "First, your eggs beat it. Then your butterflies flew. And then your bananas split?"

"You might say that," said Mrs. Bagoong, groaning.

"I just did. You've got problems, sister."

"You're telling me." Her face crumpled like an empty bag of dragonfly chips. "And almost every day since, more food has disappeared. I asked my workers and the janitors to keep an eye out. Nobody has seen anything."

Mrs. Bagoong whimpered. She sunk her face in her hands—or paws, or whatever iguanas call their front feet. I forget. She looked sadder than a wilted bowl of broccoli on a muggy day.

One thick, iguanoid tear slithered down her cheek. "If I can't stop this, I don't know what will happen. They might even fire me."

The tear did it. I can't stand to see a reptile cry.

"All right, enough of that," I said. I pulled my hat low over my eyes. "Chet Gecko is on the case. Food thieves, beware!"

She cracked a tiny smile and sniffled. I swaggered to the door and flung it open, then saluted her.

"See ya mañana, iguana."

Ba-whonk!

I'd walked into a stack of cans.

"Uh, Chet, honey? That's the pantry."

Another great exit, ruined.

2

Lookin' for Lunch
in All the Wrong Places

Once I got outside the cafeteria, I cased the joint. That's detective talk for checking the place out. Three big double doors lined the sides of the building, and on the end, a smaller door led to the kitchen. A tiny window perched above this door like a pillbox hat on a hippo.

I knew that the janitors locked up after school every day. I saw no broken locks or busted windowpanes. So, either the thief could pick locks, or it was an inside job.

I crouched down, searching the mud for footprints, secret messages, or some kind of clue. Nothing but wet dirt with wavy lines in it.

"Hiya, Chet! Trying to figure out the recipe for mud pies?"

It was my partner, Natalie Attired. The mocking-bird comedian.

"Nope, just shopping for your birthday present," I said.

She cocked her head. "What's up? We haven't had a case in weeks."

"We've got one now—a real doozy."

I told her about the food thieves. Natalie agreed to help. She eats like a bird, but she still has a soft spot for cafeteria ladies in trouble.

"So what's our first step, Mr. Detective?" she said.

"I figured we'd talk to the lunch monitors and the other cafeteria workers. Maybe they saw something they didn't tell Mrs. Bagoong about."

Just then, two lunch monitors left the cafeteria. Did I have good timing, or what?

"Hey, ladies, can I bend your ears for a minute?" I said.

The two mice looked puzzled. "I dunno. That sounds painful," squeaked the taller one.

"He means we want to talk," said Natalie.

"Oh," said the shorter one. She had a white, waxy-looking nose. "Why didn't he just say so?"

I flipped up my trench-coat collar. "I'm a private eye, that's why. Tell me, have you seen anything funny going on lately?"

"Well," said Short-and-Waxy, "yesterday, on a

bet, Nadine Rat tried to stuff seven grapes up her nose."

Tall-and-Squeaky chuckled. "Yeah, and when someone made her laugh, the grapes shot out like cannonballs!"

They giggled together.

"Not that kind of funny," I said. "We're investigating the missing food. Has anybody been snooping around?"

"Nope," said Waxy.

"Have any of the lunch crew been acting strange lately?" said Natalie.

"Nope," said Squeaky.

Two strikes. Before our investigation headed back to the dugouts, I thought I'd try pitching one more question.

"Does anyone on the lunch staff hate Mrs. Bagoong? Maybe want to get her in trouble?"

"No—wait a minute," said Squeaky. "What about Rocky Rhode?"

The two mice eyeballed each other, nervous as a pair of elephants on ice skates. They checked to make sure nobody else was listening.

"Spill the beans," I said.

They spilled.

"Rocky is the head lunch monitor," Waxy whispered. "She's tough. She fights with Mrs. Bagoong all the time."

The bell rang. Lunch period was over. The mice turned to go.

"Don't tell her we told you anything," said Squeaky.

They scurried down the hall like a couple of rodents. Typical.

"Don't worry," Natalie called after them. "We won't *rat* on you." She chuckled.

I rolled my eyes.

It wasn't much to go on, but at least we had a lead. I had crossed paths with the horned toad Rocky Rhode before. She was always guilty of something. Question was, Was she guilty of the thefts?

"How's about we go check on a certain horned toad?" I said.

"Right now?" said Natalie. "Aren't you forgetting something?"

Oh yeah.

The only problem with being a grade-school detective is you still have to go to class. Teachers won't give you time-out to solve crimes.

School is funny like that.

3

Hit the Rhode, Jack

If you want to meet roughnecks at Emerson Hicky Elementary, you visit the bike racks. Of course, most of us don't want to meet roughnecks. Most of us still have a few brain cells left.

The bike-rack gang will steal your lunch money or give you an atomic wedgie faster than a quick-draw toad zaps a mayfly. Second graders take their lives into their hands when they walk past the bike racks.

But I wasn't worried. I was a fourth-grade private eye—big and green, and full of beans.

I waited for Natalie, just in case.

We waded together through the stream of worn-out teachers and kids leaving school. And like a stream, the kids parted when they reached the bike racks.

Mugs, lugs, and killer bugs leaned or sat there, thicker than lice on a field mouse. I saw a beefy scorpion with a tattoo, two poison toads, and some other characters who put the *wild* in wildlife.

"Lookee here, it's Mr. Hotshot Private Eye." It was Erik Nidd, the giant tarantula. Erik was a real sweetheart. He'd slug me for a quarter, squash me for 50 cents, and toss me overboard in a concrete barrel for $1.75, plus sales tax.

"Well, hello, Erik," I said. "Looks like the ugly lessons are really paying off."

We had what you might call a real close relationship. If I got real close, he beat me up. If I stayed farther away, we could talk.

"What's up, gecko?" he said. "You lookin' for trouble?"

"No, I'm looking for Rocky. You seen her?"

Erik laughed, a mean snort. "Whaddaya think I am—blind?"

"No, but I think you're as sharp as an old butter knife."

"Are you trying to get smart with me?" he said.

"With you? It would take forever."

He snarled and shook two thick fists at me.

"Course I've seen her, you moron," he said. "She's sittin' right behind me."

Erik pointed one hairy leg over his shoulder. We circled him cautiously.

13

In Erik's broad shadow sat Rocky Rhode, a horned toad with a short fuse and a rap sheet as long as an elephant's suspenders. She leaned against someone's bike, carving her initials into the paint with a sharp claw.

"Hey, Rocky," I said. "Can we talk?"

She looked us over with heavy-lidded eyes.

"Go milk a duck," she said.

"It's about Mrs. Bagoong," said Natalie.

"That noodle-head? She's just lucky I don't run her out of the lunchroom."

"The way I hear it, you're not exactly her favorite lizard, either," I said.

Rocky rolled one horned shoulder. Her muscles bunched like two bobcats wrestling in a sack. "Yeah, so?"

"So, we were just wondering," said Natalie, "if you knew anything about all these food thefts in the cafeteria."

Rocky looked as coy as a T-rex with a secret boyfriend. "Beats me," she said. "But I'm not losing any sleep over it."

So much for the soft approach. I decided to try shock tactics.

"Have you been stealing food to get Mrs. Bagoong in trouble?" I said.

Rocky snarled and stood up. You might not

15

think a sixth-grade horned toad is very big. But let me tell you, it was like facing an angry cactus on steroids.

"Get this, peeper," she said. "I didn't steal the food, see? If you say I did, you're calling me a liar. Know what I do to people who call me a liar?"

She grabbed a bicycle and twisted the front tire into an abstract sculpture.

"Adopt them into your family?" I said. "Serve them Skittles and root beer?"

Rocky growled and stepped toward us. Erik turned on us, too.

"Scram, sonny boy," he said. "You too, birdie."

Some days you fight, and some days you scram. We scrammed.

Natalie and I stopped by the fence to catch our breath.

"So, what do you think?" I said. "She says she's innocent."

"Sure she is, peeper," said Natalie, in a dead-on imitation of Rocky's voice. "And Batman's really a bat, see?"

I shook my head. Fish gotta swim, mockingbirds gotta mock.

"You don't believe she didn't take the food?" I said.

"You don't believe I don't believe she didn't take the food?" she replied.

I scratched my head. "I guess you don't follow Mr. Ratnose's rule: Don't never make no double negatives."

"Not nohow."

I frowned. Sometimes Natalie's jokes go over my head. Sometimes it's just as well.

"Maybe we should tail Rocky," I said.

"She's already got a tail, Chet."

I sighed. "Tailing someone means following them around. Jeez, don't you ever watch detective movies?"

Natalie chuckled. "Gotcha, hotshot."

"I'm serious. We need a plan. Do we tail Rocky, stake out the cafeteria, or head over to my place for a snack?"

Dumb question.

Half an hour later, we sat in my backyard office, full of pizza and empty of ideas.

"We need to interview more of the cafeteria crowd," I said. "Let's do some serious legwork before school tomorrow." I thought about what I'd just said. "But not *too* early."

Natalie got up to go. She turned at the office door and raised two wing feathers in salute.

17

"See ya later, alligator," she said.

"After a while, crocodile," I said.

"Okey-dokey, artichokey."

"Till then, penguin."

"*Sayonara,* capybara."

"Uh . . . um . . ." My mind was as blank as an essay on "My Favorite Homework Assignments."

Natalie's laughter trailed off as she flew away. *Shoot.* I always hate to give a dame the last word.

4

Stainless Steal

Next morning, I met Natalie by the cafeteria. Dawn painted the treetops with pink and gold. But I didn't much care. My eyes were as blurry as an underwater chalk drawing, and my brain felt like fuzz on a lollipop.

Why can't the day start at some civilized time—say, twelve noon?

The bittersweet perfume of stinkbug muffins filled the air. The cafeteria crew was already hard at work.

"Ah, I love mornings," said Natalie. She stretched her wings wide. "Best time of the day."

I shot her a look and rapped on the kitchen door. After a couple of seconds, Mrs. Bagoong opened it. Her expression could have made plastic flowers wilt.

"Oh, it's you," she grumbled. "I thought you were going to catch those thieves."

"What, they struck again?" I asked.

"Yeah. Last night. Some detective you are!" She started to shut the door. I jammed my foot in it.

"What did they—*ow!*—take?"

Mrs. Bagoong rolled her eyes. "While you were getting your beauty sleep, they stole some more eggs and a tray of cockroach cupcakes."

Natalie leaned forward. "Did they leave any clues behind?" she asked.

"Nope, just crumbs," said Mrs. Bagoong. Her frown could have been a poster for National Bad Mood Day. But uglier.

Then she sighed and opened the door wide. "Come in and see for yourselves. For all the good it will do."

We entered the kitchen, eyes alert and noses a-sniff. She led us back to the storeroom. On the way, I detected a tray of stinkbug muffins cooling on a rack.

A private eye can never have too much breakfast.

"Come on, Chet," said Natalie. "Get your mind off food and onto detective work."

I turned to follow her. "Just checking for clues."

At first glance, the storeroom seemed unchanged. Same giant refrigerator, same tubs of food.

I looked closely at the fridge. No fingerprints.

(Of course, I couldn't have analyzed them, anyway; I was still waiting for my mail-order Dr. Fingrito Fingerprint Kit.) The metal surface was smoother than a sixth grader's lie.

I checked the storage racks inside. No clues there, either—unless you counted the locust lasagna.

"The storeroom door was locked?" asked Natalie.

"Tighter than tight," said Mrs. Bagoong. "And my assistant and I have the only keys."

I touched the doorknob. It felt slimy.

"Find something, Chet?" asked Natalie.

"No, not unless someone's picking locks with snot."

"Who nose? Maybe they just sneezed it open."
Natalie chuckled.

Natalie's puns are even worse first thing in the
morning.

Mrs. Bagoong grunted and flexed her armored
neck-plate. "Are you finished in here? I gotta get
back to work—while I still have a job."

"Tell me," I said, "what would happen if you
left? Who would take over?"

The big iguana frowned. "Minerva Stroney, I
guess. But why don't you see if you can't prevent
that?"

As we turned to go, an idea struck me. I suddenly
squatted down on the cold floor.

"You won't find any mud pies here," said Natalie.

"No, but I might find a clue. Look at this!"

I pointed at a pile of spilled flour.

Mrs. Bagoong squinted. "Ah, it's just our usual
mess. Someone got sloppy making the muffins."

She reached down to wipe up the white powder.

"Wait a minute!" I said. "I'm about to be
brilliant."

"High time," muttered Natalie.

"Let's set a trap for the thief. At the end of the
day, sprinkle flour on the floor. Then, if the thief
comes tonight, we'll see his footprints tomorrow
morning."

Mrs. Bagoong and Natalie both looked at me. Natalie cocked her head. "Not bad, partner," she said.

"It might work," said Mrs. Bagoong. Her tail twitched in excitement like a monkey doing the mambo. "I'll make sure I'm the last one to leave today. The janitors never come into the kitchen after we're gone."

"But what if the thief doesn't return tonight?" said Natalie.

"We'll just try it again," I said, "until he does."

Mrs. Bagoong frowned. "But what do we do in the meantime?"

"Keep your eye on Rocky, the lunch monitor," I said. "She's a little sneaky."

"She's a little sneaky like Julius Caesar is a little dead," said Mrs. Bagoong. "I'll watch her. What about you two?"

I tugged on my hat. "We'll be nosing around, asking questions. Oh, and that reminds me: I have a question for you."

"Yes?" said Mrs. Bagoong.

I glanced over at the stinkbug muffins. "Most detectives get a retainer when they're on a case. What about mine?"

"A retainer?" said Natalie. "Chet, you don't need to get your teeth straightened. You're a gecko."

"Not that kind of retainer, worm slurper."

Mrs. Bagoong smiled. "He wants something to cover your detective fees. And I think I know what Chet has in mind."

She lifted a couple of stinkbug muffins off the tray and handed them to us. What a princess.

"That's good for me," I said, "but what about Natalie?"

"One each," growled Mrs. Bagoong. "Don't push it."

You don't argue with a hundred-pound iguana. You just say thanks, and get back to work.

5

Messin' with Minnie Stroney

Ms. Minerva Stroney was a cook in the cafeteria, Mrs. Bagoong's second-in-command. As wide as she was tall, Ms. Stroney boasted enough warts to supply the Whangpoo Witches Choir and still have leftovers to rent out on Halloween.

But you learn to expect that from a toad.

Minerva Stroney was a whiz with soup. And her muffins weren't bad, either.

"Hey, Ms. Stroney, nice muffins," I said, around a mouthful of stinkbug muffin.

"Thanks, Chet." She looked up from her pots. "Call me Minnie."

I was hot stuff with cafeteria ladies.

"So, Minnie, we're investigating the missing food. Can you help us out?"

Minnie started slicing carrots. Dreadful vegetable.

"Well, you know I'll do whatever I can to help Mrs. Bagoong," she said, "but I just can't—" She stopped chopping vegetables and frowned. "Hmm..."

"*Hmm?*" I said. "What does that mean?"

"It means, *hmm.* I don't know if this'll help, but I saw the head lunch monitor talking to some of her rough friends yesterday."

"They do that every day," I said. "By the bike racks, after school."

"No, this was later. They were in front of the cafeteria when I saw them."

Natalie and I exchanged glances. "Did you hear what they were talking about?" she asked.

Minnie returned to her vegetables. "Not really," she said. "I was too far away. But they mentioned your name and laughed."

"*My* name?" I said.

Great. Now I was on the hit list for the school bullies.

"Anything else that could help us?" I asked.

Minnie shook her head. "Afraid not."

Natalie leaned closer. "Hey, Minnie, I've got a question for you: How do you cook an alligator?"

"I don't know. I've never tried. How *do* you cook an alligator?"

"In a Crock-Pot." Natalie squawked.

I grabbed her by a wing and towed her out of the kitchen.

"Get it?" she said. "*Crock,* as in crocodile?"

"Yeah, I get it," I said. "And you're gonna get it soon, if you don't wise up. This is a serious case."

Natalie sniffed. "*Hmph.* You're just jealous because you can't think of any puns."

I grunted and turned down the hall. Natalie was right, of course. But I wasn't about to tell her that. A private eye has his pride, after all.

The class bell rang.

"Meet you at recess," I said. "Let's tail Rocky around and see where that leads us."

"Too keen, jelly bean." Natalie grinned.

"Too absurd, mockingbird."

Detectives are no strangers to torture. Sometimes the bad guys catch you and put bamboo shoots under your fingernails. Or they tie you to a bumper and take you for a scrape around the block to make you talk.

But that's nothing compared to geometry.

I'd rather examine the angles of a case than the angles of a triangle any day. I spent an hour feeling like someone had stuffed an oversize polygon into my brain. Anything would have been a relief.

Anything except my teacher's announcement.

"Attention, class," said Mr. Ratnose, "we'll be presenting Nations of the World with the other fourth-grade classes at next week's open house."

A chorus of groans greeted this news.

"I'm dividing you into groups," said Mr. Ratnose. "Each group will make a special presentation on its country. Now, who will pass out the assignments?"

"Ooo, I'll do it, teacher," said Bitty Chu. Her buckteeth shone in an eager grin. Once a gopher, always a gopher.

I ended up in the India group, with Bitty, Shirley Chameleon, Bo Newt, and this furball we called Waldo.

"I hope we all get to wear the traditional Indian dress," said Shirley. She batted her eyes at me like a slugger swinging for a home run. "I'll help you tie your wrap."

"If you do, you'll be sari," I said.

"*Hur, hur, hur!* I get it!" said Waldo.

I prayed for recess. The only thing worse than doing a dorky project like Nations of the World was doing it with a team like mine.

I bet detective Sam Spade never had to put up with this stuff.

6

Never Sass a Sixth Grader

Recess came, sweeter than a strawberry-and-honeybee milk shake, and twice as welcome. I trotted down the halls, onto the playground, and slipped through a pack of young rodents. They were playing hopscotch and singing "Three Blind Mice."

I shook my head. No accounting for musical taste.

I found Natalie by the swings, stroking her beak and making like *The Thinker* with wings.

"I've been thinking," she said.

"Always a dangerous thing," I said.

"We need to figure out why the food is being stolen."

"Why?"

"That's what I said," she said, " 'why.' "

"No," I said, shooting her a look. "I mean, *why* do we need to figure out why the food is being stolen?"

"Oh. Because if we do that, maybe we can guess *who's* doing it."

"Oh."

We sat down on the swings and dangled our legs. It was as good a place to start as any.

"Okay," I said. "I'll bite. Why is the thief stealing food? He's hungry?"

"Or she's trying to hurt Mrs. Bagoong," said Natalie.

"Or it's throwing a party and can't afford appetizers."

I glanced over at Natalie. She wore the same expression I did—clueless as a troll on a tricycle.

"Hey, are you guys gonna swing or not?" said a scrawny frog.

"What do we look like, swingers?" I said.

He frowned.

"Bug off!" Natalie and I said together.

He bugged.

"So far, Rocky looks like our best suspect," I said. "But she acted pretty innocent yesterday—for a punk."

I stood up. Making deductions this early in a case

is harder than Chinese algebra. "Enough chitchat," I said. "Let's take a walk on the wild side."

"You mean . . . ," said Natalie.

"Yup. Time to visit the sixth graders' playground."

We headed across campus. Before long, Natalie and I leaned against a tree at the edge of the sixth-grade playground. We stood out like a chunk of broccoli in a glass of milk. But we played it cool and scanned the scene.

Funny, at first glance their playground looked a lot like ours. Same grass, same trees, same law of the jungle. Nearby, Herman the Gila Monster had a field mouse in a headlock, while Erik Nidd wove a hangman's noose.

Then I saw something that turned my stomach.

Over by the jungle gym, a couple of students twined around each other like snakes on a stick. They were making out, smooching, swapping spit.

Disgusting.

This was sixth grade? Compared to this, fourth grade was a trip to the circus in a brand-new scooter.

"Do you see Rocky?" Natalie said.

"Not yet . . . Ah, there!" Near the edge of the concrete, playing dodgeball with a pill bug, was our prime suspect: Rocky Rhode.

We watched her nail another kid with the rolled-up bug. Rocky trundled over to a low wall by the sixth-grade classroom, where Erik Nidd and some of the other roughnecks were sitting around like hood ornaments on an Uglymobile.

I leaned toward Natalie. "We've got to get closer. They could be plotting another cafeteria break-in."

Natalie and I sneaked along the line of trees toward the wall, but before we got there, Rocky's group had begun to break up. *Rats!* Too late to spy on them.

But wait. One kid stayed behind: A box turtle reading a paperback. Maybe she had heard something. We approached her.

"Hiya, sister," I said. "I'm a private eye on a case, and I sure could use some help."

She didn't even lift her eyes from the page. "Yeah?" she said. "What's it to me?"

"We're trailing a suspect named Rocky," said Natalie. "She was just here with some of her friends. Did you hear what they were saying?"

The turtle kept reading. Her neck shrank back into her shell until only her nose and eyes stuck out. "I don't remember," she said.

I slipped a quarter out of my pocket and dropped it onto the open page of her book. "Does this refresh your memory?"

Her wise eyes flashed up at me. "A quarter? I think I'm getting amnesia."

I dug in my pocket and fished out a coupon for a

discount mothburger at Bug-in-the-Box. I dropped
it next to the quarter.

The turtle sighed. "Sonny, this would go a lot
faster if you'd just made a trip to the candy machine
first." She returned to her reading.

I reached into another pocket and produced a
Three Mosquitoes candy bar I'd been saving for
snack time. I passed it before her eyes.

She moved pretty fast for a turtle. My candy bar
disappeared into her mouth, wrapper and all. She
smiled and stuck her neck out.

Chocolate works every time.

"It's a miracle," said the turtle as she munched.
"My memory's coming back. Rocky was talking
about payback time. She seemed pretty steamed at
someone, and she said she was going to 'stock up'
tonight."

Stock up? Bingo! My eyes met Natalie's. She
nodded and grinned. It sounded like Rocky was our
culprit. Lady Luck was smiling on us like a buzzard
at a carrion festival.

"Anything else?" I asked the turtle.

She spat out the candy wrapper and eyed my coat
pocket. "Any more chocolate?"

I shook my head.

"Nope, that's all," said the turtle. Her nose sunk
back into the book.

I sighed. A few more informants like this, and I'd be one hungry gecko. But it was worth it.

Natalie and I started down the hall. As we passed a classroom door, the sixth-grade teacher stuck her head out. Her mole eyes squinted behind thick glasses, and she called out.

"Wait!" said Ms. Burrower. "Have either of you seen a monster earthworm?"

Natalie and I shook our heads. "I wish," said Natalie.

"Well, if you do," said the teacher, "tell it to keep out of my tunnels. They're for moles only. No worms!"

I shot Natalie a look. Sixth grade was looking weirder and weirder.

Just then the bell rang. Can't beat that for timing.

"Duty calls," I said. "We're due back on our home planet." We trotted up the hall.

"Do you suppose she meant bookworms, too?" my partner asked.

"Natalie," I said, "That's one can of worms I don't ever want to open."

7

Kitchen Tell

By the time lunch rolled around, I knew just what to do. At least, I hoped I did. Being a private eye means taking lots of guesses and hoping they come out right.

But then, so does science class.

I shuffled along in the lunch line behind Frenchy LaTrine, a mousy cheerleader with a mouth as big as a blender and twice as fast. So far, she was using it to gossip with her friend, not to bother me. That suited me fine.

Minnie Stroney stood behind the counter, dishing out vegetables. She gave me a tight smile. "Here's some extra cauliflower, Chet. It'll help you grow."

Obviously she hadn't heard about the health secrets of the Chocolate Chip Cookie Diet.

Mrs. Bagoong stood beside Ms. Stroney. She seemed bluer than a frozen fruit fly. The queen of the lunchroom didn't even look up as she dropped a fat, greasy burrito onto my plate.

I leaned toward Mrs. Bagoong and muttered, "Tonight's the night, all right. I'll hide in the kitchen."

Ms. Stroney glanced sharply at me. She didn't say anything.

Frenchy LaTrine was another matter.

Her radar ears caught my comment, and her head swiveled like the handle on a pencil sharpener. "Why, Chet!" she said. "Isn't she a little old for you?" Her eyelashes fluttered. "Try someone your own age!"

"Right after I try cyanide pie, Frenchy," I said.

Her brow furrowed. "But... what about our relationship?"

"Keep it in your imagination, where it belongs."

She pouted, picked up her tray, and huffed away. What is it with dames? Sometimes they're nuttier than a squirrel's sundae.

I leaned back toward Mrs. Bagoong. "What time do you lock up?"

"Right after school." She sighed. "Chet, this idea of yours better work."

"It will," I said. "I'll meet you after school, and we'll set our trap. Tonight we catch a food thief!"

"Hey, Gecko," said the skink behind me. "Stop

flappin' your gums and start movin' your feet. We're starvin' here!"

I collected my tray and headed for a quiet table. I had to plan for the night's adventure. It wasn't enough to capture Rocky's footprints. I needed proof that would convince even Principal Zero.

And I thought I knew how to get it.

Natalie joined me at a sticky table in the corner. Somebody had forgotten to clean up after the kindergartners.

"So, what's our move?" she asked. "Do we stake out the kitchen tonight?"

"*I* stake out the kitchen," I said. I flicked some crab-applesauce off the table. "It's a one-gecko job."

Natalie ruffled her feathers. "But what if Rocky brings her friends? What if they catch you? You need backup."

I bit into my burrito. "They could beat up both of us, easy as one. No, we've got to use brains instead of brawn."

"So how are you going to stop them—by talking them out of it?"

I smiled. "A picture is worth a thousand words. Tell me, Natalie, does your brother still shoot photos for the school newspaper?"

When the bell rang at the end of the day, I jumped out of my seat and whistled down the hallway like gas from a stink-toad. The fewer kids who saw me sneak into the cafeteria, the better.

I rapped twice on the kitchen door. Mrs. Bagoong was waiting just inside. She looked as nervous as a hedgehog in a hang glider.

"The, uh—the trap is set," she said. "I sprinkled flour on the storeroom floor and locked the door." Mrs. Bagoong gnawed on a knuckle. "Are you sure this will work?"

"Sure as sugar," I said.

She pointed at the serving counters. "You can hide under there, and the robbers won't see you. You'll be all right?"

"Right as rain, sister. With their footprints in flour, and their mugs on film, these food thieves are as good as caught."

Just then, Natalie poked her head through the doorway. "Here's the camera, Chet. My brother says if we break it, he'll pound both of us into pudding."

I took the instamatic camera. "That's my second-favorite dessert."

Natalie cocked her head. "Are you sure you don't want me to fly home and get my walkie-talkies? I'd feel better if I could reach you."

"No worries, partner." I flipped up my coat collar. "I'll call my mom and tell her I'm sleeping over at your house. See you later tonight."

I turned to Mrs. Bagoong and gave her the thumbs-up. "We'll meet tomorrow morning. What time do you get here?"

"Six o'clock."

I shuddered. "We'll be here at seven-thirty. When you see me next, I'll have the proof we need to put those food thieves in hot water and throw away the key."

Mrs. Bagoong frowned.

"Or something like that," I said.

She and Natalie stepped outside. As the big iguana pulled the door closed, the last thing I saw was Natalie's worried face.

"Be careful, partner," she whispered.

The door locked with a click.

"No pro-blem-o," I replied.

Sure, no problem. I was only sticking my neck out farther than a giraffe with a brand-new scarf— just setting a trap for some dangerous, cold-blooded food thieves.

And hoping the trap didn't land on my tail instead.

8

Muffins of Love

With the door closed, a dim light painted the kitchen like a third-rate copy of a fourth-rate artist. The walls were drab and dingy. The metal counters gleamed coldly. All the vittles were under lock and key.

It was no place I'd want to spend my summer vacation.

I left the camera on the counter and settled onto a stool to wait.

The after-school noises swelled. Children laughing, screaming. Buses honking and pulling away. Teachers having nervous breakdowns. Slowly the sounds faded.

In the quiet, I heard the *whoosh-whoosh* of someone sweeping the hall. It drew closer and closer.

Rattle-clik.

A key slipped into the doorknob. I ducked behind the counter and held my breath.

The door opened. Somebody walked into the room, waited for a few seconds, then returned to the door. It shut with a *clack.*

A pause, then the footsteps and the *whoosh*ing broom faded like the ink on a soggy homework assignment.

Funny, Mrs. Bagoong had said that the janitors never came into the kitchen after school. Maybe someone was just checking up.

I heard the teachers' cars leaving the nearby parking lot. After that, the school fell really quiet, like a graveyard waiting for fresh stiffs. The kitchen clock ticked.

I climbed back onto a stool and looked around. The tile floors showed a modern-art gallery's worth of weird stains and splotches. The pots hung in a row, like kids waiting for detention.

I thought about the case, about Rocky. How hate had twisted her to seek revenge. But Rocky was being careless. Didn't she know we'd figure things out?

Rrrrr.

My stomach growled. Four o'clock: time for an afternoon snack. I felt in my pockets. Drat. I'd given my last candy bar to that turtle. And who knew how long it would take the food thieves to show up?

Hmm. Maybe Mrs. Bagoong had left some snacks behind. Wouldn't hurt to look.

I walked around the kitchen. Nothing on the stove . . . nothing by the racks . . . *hey!* There, on the end of the counter near the door, sat a big, fluffy pillbug muffin on a plate.

Yum, yum. How could I have overlooked that?

A note was pinned under the plate. How thoughtful. It read: *For the hardworking private eye.* No signature.

None needed. That Mrs. Bagoong had a heart as big and sweet as a chocolate water buffalo.

I tucked the note into my pocket and toasted my favorite cafeteria lady with the tasty treat. "Here's looking at you, brown eyes."

I chomped down. The crunchy pill bugs set off the texture of the fluffy muffin wonderfully. It burst with strange flavors, like my tongue's own private Fourth of July.

The muffin vanished in a minute. Too bad she hadn't left two.

I sat back down and fiddled with the camera. Had to make sure that the flash was working—it would blind Rocky and her friends while I made my escape.

Pah!

The flash went off in my face. Yup, it was working, all right. I blinked to clear my vision. Bright swirls jumped and swam before my eyes like a family of eels doing the cha-cha.

I shook my head and blinked some more, but the swirls kept on boogying.

Just then, I began to feel dizzy. The camera fell from my hand.

I felt like a spider going down the drain in a bathtub. My world spun round and round, and something dragged me down, down, down—into a pool of blackness.

The floor jumped up and hit my cheek. *How rude!* I thought. What had I ever done to the floor?

As my eyes closed, I thought I saw the kitchen door fold open. An impossibly long worm slithered through it.

Words dribbled from his mouth like a run-down tape recorder. He drawled, "Welllcommme to dreeeeamlannnd."

And the world took a nap.

9

Wake Up, Little Snoozy

It was the gentle clatter of pots and pans that awakened me. That, and the hand punching my shoulder.

"Chet, wake up!"

My head felt like a sweat sock full of mud. My tongue tasted like the inside of a warthog's nostril. And to top it off, my eyelids were stuck together like stamps in a soggy pocket.

If only I could peel them apart. . . .

A foot nudged my belly. "Wake up, you traitor!" said another voice.

That did it. Chet Gecko is no traitor. I opened my eyes to retort and found myself face-to-face with a banana peel. A talking banana peel?

Two leathery hands reached down from the skies and grabbed my coat. They pulled me up to a sitting position. I shook my head to clear it.

Mrs. Bagoong and Natalie stood before me. Their faces looked as cheerful and friendly as a get-well card from the Grim Reaper.

"Why did you do it?" said Mrs. Bagoong. "Chet, I trusted you, and this is how you repay me?"

Natalie gave me icicle eyes. "How could you? My own partner."

I could see their lips moving, but they might as well have been singing "Waltzing Matilda" backward. Their words made no sense.

Come on, Chet, get it together. Say something witty.
"Huh?" I grunted.

"Don't play dumb with me," said Mrs. Bagoong. "You're in serious trouble, mister. We're going straight to Principal Zero."

Her words still didn't make sense. She was supposed to be calling me a genius for solving the case.

I had solved it, hadn't I?

My blurry eyes scoped out the scene. I was propped against the kitchen wall, surrounded by the litter of half-eaten food. Candied butterflies, deep-fried termites, leftover burritos, banana peels, and eggshells...

Mmm. Someone had had quite a midnight snack.

And they thought it was me.

"Hang on," I said. "You don't think I—"

"Then who did?" said Mrs. Bagoong. She crossed her tree-trunk arms, looking like a linebacker in an apron. A very angry linebacker.

"I—uh, that is..." My memory was as blank as a cheerleader's eyes. "I don't know."

Natalie hopped around the mess of food. "You left enough evidence to convince a blind detective of your guilt," she said. Natalie pointed behind me.

The storeroom door gaped wide. On the floor inside was a dusting of flour, crisscrossed with... gecko footprints!

"No way!" I rolled over onto my hands and knees, and crawled to the doorsill. Yup. My footprints, all right. And long, snaky lines dragged through the flour, just like my tail would've made.

"I didn't!" I said.

"You did," said Mrs. Bagoong. "You're the food thief!"

I blinked stupidly. My brain felt like a spaceship made of cream cheese. And it was working about as well.

"Stand up," said Mrs. Bagoong. "It's time to face the music."

I planted a foot and tried to stand. It was hard. But I'm a tough guy. I did it, anyway. Then I leaned against the wall.

Natalie stepped forward with her brother's camera. She glared. "We found this in the bushes outside. My brother's going to kill you."

"Natalie, Mrs. Bagoong, listen to me. I didn't do it." I shook my head. "Honest, the last thing I remember was eating a muffin."

"You ate a lot more than that, Mr. Food Thief," growled Mrs. Bagoong.

"But you left me the muffin yourself," I said.

"*I* left you a muffin?"

"Sure," I said. I scrabbled in my pockets. "And you even wrote me a note. Here, don't you remember?"

Mrs. Bagoong looked at it and sniffed. "I didn't write that." Her neck spines bristled. "No more excuses. It's off to the principal with you. You've been a very bad gecko."

She grabbed my arm and tugged me past a scowling Minnie Stroney out the kitchen door. "March, you muffin snatcher," snarled Mrs. Bagoong.

The walk to Principal Zero's office seemed to take longer than the last day of school before vacation. Natalie sulked off to the playground. Mrs. Bagoong ignored my explanations.

We entered the office, and the principal's secretary, Maggie Crow, gave me the evil eye as I passed. Jeez, did the whole school know about it already?

Principal Zero sat behind his desk. His tail twitched, and his sharp claws kneaded the desktop like they were itching to sink into something. And that something was me.

"This time you've gone too far, Gecko," he purred. Somehow, his smile was scarier than his frown. "And this time I'm going to throw the book at you."

I gulped. "Mr. Zero, it's not what it looks like. I didn't really eat all that food."

"Oh, no?" he said.

"No. You see, I was working on a case, and the suspect got the drop on me. I was framed."

Mr. Zero's eyes narrowed to slits. "You always have a smooth answer ready, don't you?"

"What do you want me to do?" I said. "Learn to stutter?"

"Your wisecracks won't help you now, Gecko. You can't talk your way out of this."

He tossed an envelope across his desk. I slipped a note and two photos from it.

"Someone left that under my door this morning," said Principal Zero.

The note read, *Chett Gekko did it!* and it was signed, *N. Igma.*

Sweat popped out on my forehead. Or it would have, if geckos could sweat.

I looked at the first photo and laughed in relief. It was the shot I accidentally took when testing the flash. "I can explain. It was an accident."

"I'll bet," said the principal dryly. "It takes a pretty dumb thief to photograph himself."

"But this doesn't—"

I scanned the second shot, and my breath stuck in my throat like a stale doughnut. There I was, in living color, with my feet in the flour and a feast on the floor.

"Say your prayers, Gecko," said Principal Zero. "You're going down."

10

Photo Finished

I sank to my knees on the thick carpet. *Not possible!* my brain kept shouting. And yet, there I was in a color photo, caught in the act of robbing the storeroom.

"It's a fake," I whispered.

I gulped. Someone had framed me better than the priciest Picasso in the national museum. Was it Rocky? I had to find out.

"Chet Gecko," said Mr. Zero, "I should suspend you from school for stealing food." He smoothed the fur on his jowls. "But I'm not going to do that."

I looked up in surprise. "You're not?"

"No, it wouldn't be right."

Principal Zero smiled broadly. A white fang

twinkled. "Instead of suspending you, I'm going to give you detention . . . for life."

I felt as bouncy as a dodgeball after it meets a rusty nail. "De-detention . . . ," I stuttered.

"'For life,'" said Mrs. Bagoong. "Principal Zero, that's the perfect punishment. You've been most fair. Although . . ."

She looked up at the ceiling, considering something. Would the queen of the cafeteria grant me some mercy?

Principal Zero leaned forward. "Yes?"

"Maybe you could add on a few years of dishwashing duty at lunchtime?"

"Done," he said. My principal scribbled something on a pink slip, then tore it off the pad. "Take this to your teacher," he told me. "I want everyone to know of your shame."

I took the slip with a shaky hand and stood up with even shakier legs. This was a tight spot, no mistake. Tighter than a tapeworm's T-shirt.

It would take some topflight detective work to get me off the hook and get the goods on Rocky, or whoever the real thief was. I hoped I was up to it.

I hoped I could convince Natalie to help me.

Mrs. Bagoong opened the door and I sleepwalked through the office into the hall. As I stumbled to my classroom, I found only one cheering thought (other than picturing an asteroid hitting the planet before my mom found out).

I thought, *Maybe this frame-up will make Mr. Ratnose drop me from our stupid open-house project.*

I should have known better.

"Are you kidding?" said Mr. Ratnose. He crumpled the pink slip. His ears flattened against his head. "You think a lousy excuse like this will get you out of doing your Nations of the World project? Think again, mister."

"But—"

He tossed the note into his wastebasket. "I don't care if you stole the *Mona Lisa* and painted *hootchy mama!* on it. Open house is on Monday, and you're playing Mr. India. Now, sit down and study, *sahib.*"

This was shaping up to be one of those days when I wished I'd joined the French Foreign Legion instead of coming to school.

I trudged back to my seat. Word had got around. My classmates were whispering and pointing at me.

More than they usually do, I mean.

Shirley Chameleon leaned over. "Oh, Chet," she whispered, "it's so tragic that you've turned to a life of crime. What drove you to it—unrequited love?"

She batted her eyes. Actually, she batted one eye

while the other one watched the teacher. Chameleons are creepy that way.

Her face drew closer to mine. "If there's anything I can do to help...anything at all," she said. If Shirley got any nearer, she'd be wearing my T-shirt.

"Yeah, there's one thing you can do," I said. "Take your cooties back into your own seat and give them a rest."

Dames. Whether they think you are a good boy or a bad boy, they always spell trouble.

And just then, I had enough trouble to last until high school.

11

The Frame Game

After math class, our study groups met to work on the Nations of the World fiasco. At the open house next Monday, we were supposed to dress in dorky costumes and talk about our assigned countries.

Before then, we had to learn something about the country. And that meant studying—my favorite activity, next to watching a mole's nose hairs grow. All I knew about India was that it had people with flutes who charmed snakes.

And right then, the only person I wanted to charm was my partner—into working with me to solve the case.

But we read our books, and blathered on about our presentation. Until, finally, I heard the sweet sound of freedom.

Rrring! went the recess bell.

I was up and out the door quicker than a cheetah on a coffee break. First thing, I had to find Natalie and get her to help me.

My stomach growled.

Okay, second thing. Being knocked out all night and missing meals sure gives a private eye an appetite.

Luckily, I had some spare change in my pockets. A box of Sugar Frosted Ladybugs from the vending machine would take the edge off my hunger.

I plugged my coins into the machine. As I bent to pick up the candy, a voice behind me said, "Oh, it's you."

I turned. Natalie had already begun to leave.

"Natalie, wait."

She stopped, her back to me. "Yeah?"

"Partner, I didn't do it," I said. "You've got to believe me."

Natalie ruffled her tail feathers. "Why should I?" she said. "All the evidence points to you."

I walked around to face her. "What are you going to believe? The evidence or your partner?"

"Good point." She turned to go.

"Natalie, I was framed."

"Prove it," she said.

"I can, if you help me. Look, I'm starving now," I said. I wolfed down the Sugar Frosted Ladybugs.

"Would I be so hungry if I'd eaten all that food?"

Natalie looked pointedly at my gut. "Yes."

I grimaced. "Okay, bad example. But that photo was faked, and if we can find it, I'll show you."

Natalie narrowed her eyes.

I swallowed my pride. It wasn't as tasty as the ladybugs.

"Please, Natalie. I can't do it without you."

That did it. Natalie likes to know she's indispensable.

"Okay, I'll help," she said. "But if it turns out you're lying, I'll never speak to you again."

I grinned. "Promise?"

She glared.

"Just kidding, just kidding," I said.

I led the way down the halls toward Principal Zero's office.

Natalie asked, "Uh, Chet? Where are we going?"

"To snatch those photos from the principal's office."

Natalie smirked. "I don't recommend it."

"Why not?" I said. "How else can I prove I'm innocent?"

"Try visiting the library."

The library? She walked off. I followed her, with my brain full of questions and my mouth full of ladybug aftertaste. Kinda crunchy.

Natalie pushed through the library doors and walked up to the bulletin board. "Here you go," she said.

Someone had posted the photo on the main bulletin board. It didn't show my good side. Together, Natalie and I studied the picture.

"Looks pretty bad, Chet," said Natalie. "I swear, if you're lying—"

"Hang on," I said. "What's this?"

In the photo, my eyes were closed and I was wearing a wide belt around my waist. I touched my waist and felt a sticky spot—probably leftover banana goop—but no belt.

"Natalie, I *never* wear a belt. What's that?" I pointed at the picture. She bent closer.

"Hey," she said, "you're right. And look at the floor. I see your footprints in the flour, but there're too many wavy lines for just your tail prints."

"What's going on?" I said.

"That's what I'd like to know," a low voice snarled behind me.

We whirled around. It was Mrs. Toaden, my dreaded first-grade teacher. "Are you admiring your handiwork, or just trying to add to your crimes?" she hissed.

"What do you mean?" I asked.

Old Toady pointed a sharp-clawed finger at the library wall, where the sign says QUIET, PLEASE. She shook the finger at us. "Are you looking for worse punishment?"

"Worse than repeating your class?" I said. "Not in this lifetime. Come on, Natalie."

As we passed through the doors and hit the playground, Natalie admitted, "You're right; something's fishy. How can I help?"

"Come with me," I said. "We're going to talk with someone we should have seen at the beginning."

Silly me. I had forgotten the first rule of the school yard: If you want to get in trouble, ask the principal; if you want to know what's going on, ask the janitor.

12

Grime War

I rapped on the office door of Maureen DeBree, head janitor at Emerson Hicky. Ms. DeBree knew the name of every candy wrapper that fell at our school, and who dropped it. Not a wad of gum was stuck to a desk without her knowing—and catching—the culprit.

Some kids said she had trash radar.

The door opened. There she stood, with tool belts slung across her narrow chest like bandoliers. Her bright eyes twinkled watchfully, and her fuzzy mongoose ears twitched.

Maureen DeBree was a warrior in the battle against grime. Even her bushy tail had a sponge attachment.

"Whassup, kids?" she rasped. Natalie and I got a whiff of ammonia strong enough to build a house on. It was rumored that Ms. DeBree drank it straight, with a twist of lemon and a WD-40 chaser.

She wasn't squeaky, but she was clean.

"We're on a case and we need your help," I said. "I've been framed for the cafeteria food thefts. We think Rocky Rhode is guilty, but we can't prove it."

Ms. DeBree wrinkled her nose and rubbed her paws together thoughtfully. "Stealing food, eh? That's one serious charge."

"Have you seen anything at all that could help us?" I asked.

Ms. DeBree motioned us into her room. Mops, buckets, and brooms stood at attention along two walls. Canisters of gas—propane, helium, laughing—were ranked against another wall. Bottles of ammonia and polish were lined up like good soldiers.

Ms. DeBree was just a few products shy of opening her own warehouse outlet.

She upended a gleaming bucket and planted herself on top of it.

"Detective, eh?" she said, eyeing me. "Let me tell you, searching for the truth is a tricky business. Don't want to take any wrong turns or cast nasturtiums on anybody."

Natalie leaned closer. "You mean, cast aspersions?" That Natalie and her vocabulary words. "Do you know something?" she asked Maureen DeBree.

"Do I *know* something? Nah," said the mongoose. I slumped.

"But do I *suspect* something?" she said. "You betcha."

My head snapped up. "What is it? Something about Rocky?"

Ms. DeBree sucked thoughtfully on an old Q-tips swab. "Can't say. But check out what I found in the bushes by the cafeteria last week."

She reached for a trash bag on a low shelf. Opening it, the mongoose fished out the longest snakeskin I'd ever seen. You could carpet a three-bedroom house with it and still have enough left over for furniture doilies.

Her lip curled in a sneer. "Cobra." She spat. "We got a dirty rotten cobra on campus. There's nothing I hate more worse."

Natalie and I exchanged a puzzled look. The cobra couldn't be a student, because no poisonous or constricting snakes were allowed at Emerson Hicky. Not since the El Monte Python Incident.

"But what does a cobra have to do with the thefts?" I said. "Is Rocky in cahoots with a poisonous snake?"

"How could she be in Cahoots," said Natalie in

a Groucho Marx voice, "when she's here with us at Emerson Hicky?"

I shot her a deadpan look. Mockingbirds can be a pain sometimes.

Ms. DeBree scratched behind her ear. "Beats me. You're the detectives; use your powers of reduction."

"That's *deduction*," I said absently. I didn't see the snakeskin's connection to my case, but a detective can never have too many clues. I thanked Ms. DeBree, and we turned to go.

"Hang on," said the mongoose. "Ain't you gonna ask me, have I seen anything else suspicious? Cheez, what kine detective are you, anyway?"

I turned and gave her my serious frown. "So," I said. "Seen anything else suspicious?" Gotta keep your sources happy.

Ms. DeBree leaned back and smiled. "Yeah, as a matter of fact. We got something more worse than food thieves. We got ghosts."

"Ghosts?" said Natalie.

I stroked my chin. Maybe Maureen DeBree had slurped one too many ammonia cocktails. "What gives you that idea?" I said.

"After school, lately I been hearing voices," said Ms. DeBree. Her ears twitched. "High, whispery kine voices."

Natalie and I looked at each other. I raised an eyebrow. "Have you talked to the school nurse?" I asked.

"Naw," said Ms. DeBree, "only to the voices. But they never talk back. It's the strangest thing."

Natalie and I backed out the door slowly. It's never a good idea to spook a mongoose gone mental.

Maureen DeBree stood and called after us. "Hey, maybe the ghosts is taking the food. Maybe we got one of them—what-you-call—poultrygeists."

We waved good-bye and started up the hall.

Natalie cocked her head. "What did all that have to do with Rocky?"

"Beats me," I said. "Hey, can you ask around at lunchtime, find out Rocky's whereabouts yesterday afternoon?"

"What about you?"

I shook my head. "I've got a date with Mrs. Bagoong."

Natalie narrowed her eyes. "That reminds me," she said. "You've got a date with my brother, too. He wants to talk to you about what happened to his camera."

The bell rang. Recess was done—as done as my career, unless I could piece together some of these strange clues.

"Tell him to get in line," I said, and shuffled off to my next torment: history class.

13

Dishwater, Dishwater Everywhere

All through history class I puzzled over the clues. Mr. Ratnose droned on and on about the Protestant Deformation and the Spanish Armadillo (or something like that; I wasn't paying much attention).

I just pasted a good-student look on my face and let my mind run like a hamster at a fox convention.

How had Rocky stolen the food from a locked room, and framed me? What was her connection, if any, to Ms. DeBree's mysterious cobra?

And how the heck was I going to buy lunch without any lunch money? (That last question worried me most of all.)

After the lunch bell rang, I sleepwalked into the cafeteria, still wrapped up in my problems. I had a rude awakening.

Someone snarled, "You! I got a bone to pick with you." Rolling toward me like a horned tank was Rocky Rhode.

"Oh yeah?" I sneered. "Which bone you wanna pick, your nose bone?"

I've never been one to pass up a wisecrack, even in the face of a serious bruising.

Kids near us scooted back to form a half circle. They grinned expectantly. Nothing like a lunchroom brawl to quicken their hearts, the little angels.

Rocky circled me like a string around a yo-yo. Her horns bristled. "What's the big idea, nosing around, telling everyone I'm stealing food? You're cruisin' for a bruisin', Gecko."

No matter the situation, a trained detective always keeps his cool.

I lost mine.

"Nice try, you cockroach-muncher," I said. My tail twitched as I orbited Rocky. "But it won't work. You framed me, and you're taking the fall for your crime."

Rocky snorted and flexed her spiny shoulders. "Framed you?" she said. "Bucko, when I'm finished with you, you won't fit in a frame. They'll have to use a spatula."

Just then, two scaly paws grabbed me from behind and hoisted me into the air. A voice reeking of garlic potato bugs snarled in my ear.

"Chet Gecko, you've gone from thief to bully in one day," said Mrs. Bagoong. "Leave my lunch monitor alone and eat your lunch. It's on me. I want you nice and strong for dish-washing."

Rocky gave me the evil eye, but she turned and trundled off. She knew that fighting in front of Mrs. Bagoong was about as smart as playing Marco Polo with piranhas.

The queen of the lunchroom set me down. She swatted me toward the lunch line.

"Eat!" said Mrs. Bagoong. "Then report to the kitchen sink in ten minutes. Your tush is *mine*."

She didn't need to tell me twice. Ah well, at least we were still on speaking terms.

If you called that speaking.

I scarfed down my food, keeping an eye out for Rocky and her friends. I didn't even notice what was on my plate—a first for Chet Gecko.

Ten minutes later, I stood by a sink full of soapy water and awaited my punishment.

Whomp!

Mrs. Bagoong dumped a stack of dirty trays right by the sink. It loomed over me like the Leaning Tower of Pizza Crusts.

Whap!

She slapped a pair of scummy rubber gloves into my hand.

"Wash!" said Mrs. Bagoo[...]

"What, no pep talk?" I [...]
stomped off.

I put my wit on hold. S[...]
she'd like hearing that privat[...]
rolled up my sleeves, put o[...]
rinsing crud off the trays.

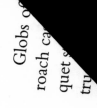

grease, stinkweed beans, spoiled cock‑
serole, and harsh soap blended into a bou‑
trong enough to knock a horsefly off a garbage
ck. I tried to breathe through my mouth, but
greasy soapsuds landed on my tongue.

Yuck.

If I didn't solve this case soon, I'd be facing life as a school outcast with prune fingers and body odor straight from the city dump. What I needed was a break in the case, some good grades in math, or a long vacation on a warm beach.

What I got was another confusing clue.

14

Everybody Needs a Ladle Love

The line of kids at the counter had trickled out. Mrs. Bagoong was keeping order in the lunchroom with a pretty big spatula and a pretty ugly expression.

Ms. Stroney wiped her hands on her apron and headed past me, deeper into the kitchen. Her bulging eyes shot me a funny look—pity mixed with amusement and a dash of contempt.

Maybe it was my winning personality, maybe it was just my stench.

Pssssss!

A loud hissing came from somewhere near the back door, like a busted teakettle trying to learn to whistle. Minnie Stroney rushed to the door and cracked it just enough to look out.

"Are you crazy?" said Ms. Stroney to whoever was outside. "What are you doing here?"

From where I stood, I couldn't hear the response. I took a couple of steps toward the door.

If only I could hear the other half of this one-sided conversation. . . .

Bap!

A speeding spatula collided with my fanny.

"Chet Gecko! Back to your post!" shouted Mrs. Bagoong in my ear. I jumped like a toad rocket. Iguanas sure can move quietly when they want to.

Mrs. Bagoong turned to her cook. "Minerva, give me a hand with those dirty trays. Hop to it!"

Minnie Stroney slammed the door and hopped. I grabbed another slimy tray and plunged it into the soapy water. From the corner of my eye, I watched Ms. Stroney bring a new stack of trays to the sink.

"So," I said casually, "who was that?"

The cook's eyelids dropped like the curtain on a third-rate magic act. She studied me through slits. "Who was what?" she said, even more casually.

I jerked my head toward the door. "Your visitor."

Her wide mouth tightened. "Oh, just my ex-boyfriend," said Ms. Stroney. "What a pest."

She hustled back into the lunchroom.

Hmm. I mused as I rinsed. Was there more to

Minnie Stroney than met the eye? Or was I so des-
perate, I was scraping the barrel for suspects?

One thing I knew: If the other private eyes found
out I had dishpan hands, I'd be laughed out of the
profession. It was time to make my move.

If only I knew what move to make.

15

Necessity Is the Mother of Detention

Maybe it was my imagination, but back in the classroom Shirley Chameleon seemed to slide her desk a little farther from mine. At least there were some fringe benefits to smelling like a trash heap.

I brooded over my situation while the afternoon passed as sweetly and gently as a nightmare in a dentist's chair. And as for my classes—well, they were classes. What can I say?

At last, the final bell rang. I hopped from my seat and pushed through my classmates toward the door.

"Don't forget," yelled Mr. Ratnose, "open house is Monday. Be prepared!"

School was over for the week. The halls swelled with babbling students bouncing off walls, driven mad by the thought of a weekend's freedom. But my spirits were lower than an earthworm's belly button.

I trudged toward the cafeteria, thinking to nose around for some clues. Then I heard something that made my spirits dive even lower.

"There you are!" rasped a buzz-saw voice. It sounded like someone who wanted to be feared and usually got what she wanted.

I whirled and found myself staring up at the Beast of Room 3, Ms. Glick. From the tips of her red-painted claws to the top of her pillbox hat, she was trouble, pure and simple. And detention hall was her own private theme park of evil.

Ms. Glick showed me a toothy alligator smile as phony as a first grader's forged permission slip. "Did you forget about detention, Mr. Gecko?" she said. "Remember, you and I are going to be close friends for quite a while."

Sure we were. And parents really mean it when they say, *This is going to hurt me more than it does you.*

"Why, Ms. Glick," I said. "What a treat. I was just wrapping up some business before stopping by."

The Beast of Room 3 thrust her sharp snout in my face and gave me an educational close-up of her dental work. "When you have detention with me, you come straight to my room after class. Remember that, mister."

"I'll tie a string around my finger," I said.

She growled deep in her throat, a sound like Bigfoot's belly digesting a small bear. I had pushed things as far as I could.

My shoulders slumped. "Lead on," I said.

I followed Ms. Glick's broad scaly back as she plowed down the hall, parting kids and teachers like a sword through butter. As we neared Room 3, Natalie appeared at my elbow.

"You'll never guess what I found out," she muttered from the side of her mouth.

"What?" I whispered back.

Ms. Glick wheeled on us. "Zip your lip, Gecko," she said. The Beast of Room 3 fixed her beady eyes on Natalie. "And no fraternizing with the prisoner."

She turned and waddled through the door. I whispered to Natalie, "Call me tonight."

Natalie leaned forward. "But Chet, it's about—"

"Gecko!" snarled Ms. Glick.

I sighed and shuffled into Room 3. Only a handful of prisoners—er, students—huddled inside its booger green walls today. A bedraggled hamster, a sneering turtle, a couple of evil little weasels . . .

And over by the windows, my new best friend, Rocky Rhode. The look in her eyes would've melted a concrete vest.

Ms. Glick pointed a thick claw at a chair two

seats behind Rocky. "Park your carcass, mister," she told me.

I parked. It was the scenic side of the room. Rusty heating vents lined the wall, and the floor tiles featured clever graffiti from earlier captives.

Detention bites! read one comment. *Glick is thick* read another. It wasn't Shakespeare, but it got the point across.

I felt a laser burning a hole in the top of my head. I glanced up. It was Rocky, sending me her meanest evil eye.

"Eyes front, Miss Rhode," said the Beast of Room 3. "Do your homework."

Rocky slowly turned back around. When Ms. Glick returned to her stack of test papers, I slipped a short carton of chocolate milk from my pocket. I'd found a fringe benefit to working in the cafeteria.

I chugged the carton. *Smooth.* That chocolate milk had been keeping the right company.

I eyed the clock. Fifty minutes to go.

I twiddled my thumbs. I counted the ceiling tiles. I actually considered doing homework. If this kept up for too long, I'd go stir crazy.

Detention sure puts a crimp in detective work.

"Pssst!" A faint hiss drew my gaze out the open window. It was Natalie. She mouthed, "Read this," and lofted a paper airplane at me.

Just in time, I snatched it from the air.

Ms. Glick's head snapped up. "What was that?"
"Just a fly," I said. "I'm saving it for a snack."

The Beast of Room 3 harrumphed and went back to writing big red F's on test papers. I waited until the coast was clear, then unfolded Natalie's airplane. It read:

CHET—
Rocky didn't do it. Coach Stroganoff says she was at soccer practice all yesterday afternoon. He made her run laps until sundown because she nailed him with water balloons.

Rocky, *innocent*? My jaw dropped. That was like saying fire is wet or vice principals just want to help you.

If it was true, that meant Rocky had been after Coach Stroganoff, not Mrs. Bagoong. And she'd been stockpiling water balloons, not food.

That put me back at square one with a pocket full of mismatched clues and a brain throbbing with one question: If Rocky wasn't stealing food, then who the heck was?

16

Just Ghost to Show You

I sat in detention like a wart on a toad, bloated and useless. My mind was as blank as a blackboard after the teacher's pet gets through with it.

A gnat circled my head. I let it.

Through my daze, I heard a long faint hiss. I glanced out the window again, but Natalie had gone.

I scanned the room and sniffed. If someone was passing gas, they had mastered their stealth technique. But I couldn't smell anything.

Ms. Glick was still punishing her stack of test papers. My fellow prisoners huddled alone, sunk in their own blue funk.

The hissing continued.

Was it coming from the heating vents? I bent closer, and the hissing resolved itself into whispers.

"More, get me more," said one speaker.

"Not tonight," said a lower voice. "Ssshhe won't help usss anymore."

Ghosts? With speech impediments? I pinched myself, but I wasn't dreaming. Maybe Maureen De-Bree wasn't a mental mongoose after all.

Or maybe I was starting to crack up, too.

"I'm almossst ready, but I need more," said the higher voice.

"Monday. I'll sssneak in when they're all dissstracted. It'll be unlocked."

I eased from my seat and leaned closer to the vent.

"Chester Gecko," said Ms. Glick. I hate it when they use my full name. "If you don't have enough to do, I could give you something."

"Don't bother, teacher."

The Beast of Room 3 gave me her best beauty-queen smile, the one that looked like a mouthful of broken glass and razor blades.

"No bother at all," she said sweetly. "Come up here and write something on the blackboard for me. How about, oh, *I will not roam about the room while being punished*? One hundred times should do nicely."

I shuffled to the front of the room. Maybe I could talk my parents into moving to a new town.

Preferably one without an elementary school.

Somehow, detention passed. The sun sank. Dinner came and went. My life rolled on.

But somehow, too, the sunset looked like a muddy smear, and my plate of termites au gratin tasted like a plumber's handkerchief. This case was getting to me.

All weekend, I worried. It didn't help that school was locked up tight, and I couldn't even investigate my own belly button.

I bet grown-up detectives never have to face problems like this. Childhood is heck.

Just before school Monday morning, I met Natalie by the flagpole.

I squinted at the early sun peeking over the hill.

Morning had broken. And I hoped they'd never get around to fixing it.

"What's wrong?" said Natalie. "You look like you haven't slept since Friday."

I waved her off. "Nothing a few Cockroach Clusters couldn't cure. Let's get down to business. Are you sure Rocky is innocent?"

"As sure as a worm is chewy," she said. "Rocky may hate your guts, but she's no food thief."

We wandered toward the playground. I told Natalie about hearing the ghosts in detention.

Her eyes grew big. "Wow," she said. "Our school is haunted? Cool."

"But why would ghosts need to wait for a door to be unlocked? Can't they just walk through walls?"

Natalie cocked her head. "*Hmm.* Maybe we've got thick ghosts. Or maybe they need a skeleton key."

Even for Natalie, that was a weak joke.

I groaned. "Think. What would a ghost be wanting more of?"

"Huh?"

"One ghost said it wanted more, and that it was almost ready. Ready for what?"

"Something *spook*-tacular?" Natalie grinned.

I glared.

"Okay, okay," she said. "I'll stop trying to cheer

you up. Let's see. . . . What do ghosts want—soul food?"

The morning bell put an end to our detective work. Just as well. I felt as sharp as a spaghetti noodle.

Whoever had framed me, they'd covered their tracks well. I was fresh out of suspects and grasping at ghosts.

And to top it off, tonight was open house—show time for our stupid Nations of the World presentation. I almost wished the ghosts would scare off our audience.

As I trudged to class, I realized that Shakespeare had it right: A Monday by any other name would still stink.

17

A Hiss Is Just a Hiss

Morning classes crawled by like they'd been stuck to flypaper with superglue. We rehearsed our open-house presentation.

Oh joy.

As a snake charmer, I wore a turban and played a flute, while Shirley, Bitty, and Bo recited a poem about India. Furball Waldo was the snake.

We sat down. From the corner of my eye, I watched the clock stagger toward recess time like a three-legged dingo in a snowbank.

"*Psst.* Chet?" It was Shirley. She fiddled with her scarf and smiled. "I thought maybe we could practice again during recess. I want things to be just right for tonight."

Yeah, sure. I needed another dose of her cooties like I needed a lifetime supply of broccoli.

The bell rang.

I tipped my hat. "Sorry, sister. Duty calls."

She gave me her best pout, the one that makes her daddy want to slip out his wallet and buy toys. I slipped out the door instead.

My feet carried me to Maureen DeBree's office. She wasn't there, so I hoofed it down the halls to find her.

"Wait up, partner!" Natalie called. "Where ya headed?"

I slowed as she flapped up to me. "Gotta see a janitor about a ghost," I said.

"Count me in."

Natalie and I covered the campus like mud on a warthog's belly. We found seven second graders singing, five first graders frolicking, and a fat partridge stuck in a pear tree.

But no janitor.

"Hey, Chet," said Natalie. "What do we do with the ghosts if we catch them—have you thought of that?"

I mused as we moseyed past the swings. "It's been haunting me all weekend, partner."

Natalie groaned. I shook my head when I realized what I'd said.

Unconscious punning—definitely not a good sign.

We found Ms. DeBree at the edge of the playground. She was spearing crumpled milk cartons with her trash spike and muttering to herself. The world's cleanest janitor nodded as we approached.

"Eh, you kids ever catch that food-napper?" asked Maureen DeBree.

"Still working on it," I said. "Listen, I heard two ghosts talking on Friday—through the heating vents. Have you heard any more from them?"

Ms. DeBree stuffed the milk cartons into her trash bag. Her ammonia perfume was strong enough to make my eyes water at five paces.

"Not me. They been as quiet as a moose," she said. "But look what I find today."

The wiry mongoose dug into her trash bag and produced a scrap of snakeskin. The hair on her shoulders stood on end and her lip curled in a snarl as she held up the dried skin between two fingers.

"Another snake?" said Natalie.

Maureen DeBree nodded grimly. "Two cobras. And you know what that means?"

"Four more and they'll have a snake six-pack," I said impatiently. "Look, let's get back to the ghosts and—"

"*Hmph!*" said the janitor. "And you call yourself a

private eyeball!" She dropped the snakeskin back into her bag and sprayed her hands with disinfectant. "Two stinking cobras means a stinking cobra nest somewheres . . . and lots of little stinking baby cobras."

Ms. DeBree wheeled and set off across the playground. "I gotta find 'em quick," she said over her shoulder. "Or we get some big trouble."

The class bell rang. Natalie and I looked blankly at each other.

"Our school is crawling with cobras, ghosts, and food thieves," I said. "We're up to our elbows in mysteries, and look at me. Where am I going?"

"Back to class," said Natalie.

I sighed. It isn't easy being a grade-school detective.

18

As the Worm Turns

What with classes, dish-washing, and detention, Natalie and I didn't have a chance to talk until open house began. All fourth-grade classes met in the cafeteria, where rows of folding chairs had been set up. Smiling parents and frowning little brothers and sisters filled the metal seats.

I was straightening my turban when Natalie plopped into the seat beside me. She adjusted her tail feathers.

"Chet, I've been thinking," she said.

"This isn't about that quarter I owe you, is it?"

Natalie raised an eyebrow. "Do you remember anything from your night in the kitchen? Something that might tell us who gave you that knockout muffin?"

I scratched my chin. I ransacked my mind like a midnight raid on the fridge. No use. All I found were soggy fragments of memories. Leftovers.

"Nope," I said. "I remember getting dizzy, dropping the camera . . ." Natalie shot me a look. "Sorry. Anyhow, I hit the floor and everything got foggy."

Natalie frowned. "You don't remember a voice, a face . . . anything?"

I closed my eyes. Nothing to see but those funny little specks swimming like worms in the darkness. Wait a minute—*worms?*

My eyes snapped open. "I *do* remember something." I pointed toward the kitchen at the back of the cafeteria. "Just as I blacked out, I saw a really long worm coming through that kitchen door."

"*Mmm,* wish I'd been there," said Natalie dreamily. She caught herself. "I mean, uh, a *worm*? Why would a worm steal food?"

"Beats me," I said. "I thought they ate dirt."

But before we could take it any further, Mr. Ratnose started the show.

The auditorium fell dark, except for the stage lights. Then, my teacher marched to the microphone, whiskers all atwitter, wearing a hat that sprouted the flags of all nations.

For a rat, he was quite a ham.

"Welcome, dear parents," said Mr. Ratnose, "to

the fourth graders' amazing, amusing presentation. May I introduce, for your entertainment pleasure, the Nations of the World!"

The first group of kids got up, dressed in leather shorts and carrying a sausage as big as a sea serpent. An armadillo recited: "'In Germany our knees are frozen / 'cause we wear our lederhosen.'"

And our show went downhill from there.

Somehow, the presentation lurched and staggered toward its ending. I've seen better acting from my little sister at bedtime. But the audience sat there goo-goo eyed, drinking in every word. *Parents.*

My group walked onstage to present India. Shirley cleared her throat and read from a scrap of paper: "'In India we do suggest / you'll find our curried shakes the best!'"

But, corny as our piece was, it couldn't keep my mind off of the case. As I fiddled around with the flute, I kept thinking, *If a worm is the food thief, how did it cook that knockout muffin without any hands? And how did it open the doors?*

My mind wandered like a doodlebug in a department store. Then, two things happened.

First, I noticed the cafeteria ladies sitting together, over to one side. And it struck me like a lunch tray to the chops: The food theft *was* an inside

job! Someone had unlocked the doors for the giant worm—and it wasn't Rocky.

So that meant one of two people: Mrs. Bagoong, or her second-in-command, Minnie Stroney—the muffin whiz. I gasped.

Shirley turned one eye on me. "Uh, Mr. Snake Charmer?" she said. "Are you all right?"

And then, the second thing happened. I saw, behind the audience, a long, crooked shape crawling through the dim kitchen. I stuffed my flute in my belt and leaped off the stage.

"Come on, Natalie," I cried. "Time to catch a food thief!"

Heads turned as I rushed down the aisle toward the kitchen, with Natalie close behind. I stepped past the food counter and reached for the light switch, shouting, "Freeze, you worm!"

The sudden glare of overhead lights revealed . . . a huge cobra! With his tongue wrapped around the doorknob of the storeroom!

"Eeee!" the audience screamed.

I acted before thinking. Not a good idea.

"Yaah!" I jumped onto the cobra's back and grabbed him tightly around the neck.

Thhwipp! The cobra's tongue slipped back into his mouth like a sword in a scabbard. The massive snake turned and slithered toward the half-open kitchen door.

I hung on with hands and feet. As we glided past an astonished Natalie, I shouted, "Quick! Go get Ms. DeBree. I'll slow him down."

"How?" she said.

I had no idea.

But I knew one thing for sure: Getting *on* a cobra is much easier than getting off.

19

Snakes Alive!

I clung to the cobra's back like ugly on an ape. He twisted around to bite me, but I was riding too high up on his neck.

I pulled back on his hood like a horse's reins. "Whoa, snakey! Whoa, there."

It had about as much effect as tickling a boulder.

Without breaking his fast slither, the snake hissed, "The name'sss not Sssnakey. It'sss Jimmy King."

That voice! I knew it in an instant. This was one of the "ghosts" I'd heard through the heater vents in detention.

He glided through the shadows like a dark river, and I watched Natalie flap off to find Ms. DeBree. That mongoose would fix his wagon.

If only I could slow him down long enough for her to catch up.

"Can't we stop and talk this over?" I said.

The cobra whipped along like a warp-speed roller coaster. "What'sss to dissscusss?" he said. "We're moving in."

I gripped his undulating body like a chocoholic clings to a candy bar. I started to feel seasick. "Bu-but Principal Zero wou-wouldn't like that."

"Who caressss? When the eggsss hatch, I'll fill the hallsss of this ssschool with my children—they'll be the sssmartesssst sssnakesss in the world!"

At least Jimmy King Cobra wasn't sssuffering from low self-esteem. And he wasn't slowing down, either. The snake zipped down the halls toward . . . the boiler room?

He executed a quick roll, trying to scrape me off.

Ooof! I felt like the bottom dog in a dog pile, but I held on.

My turban unrolled behind me, littering the hall like a toilet-paper streamer. And then it struck me: I was a snake charmer! (Or, at least, I played one on the stage.)

I fumbled in my costume belt for the flute. Still there.

We were closing fast on the half-open boiler-room door.

One-handedly, I stuck an end of the flute into my mouth and started to blow. Amazingly, it worked.

The cobra slowed, a few feet shy of the door. His pointed snout turned toward me, his eyes narrowed. "Take sssome lessonsss!" he hissed.

Jimmy King Cobra cracked his body like a bullwhip.

And I went flying.

Unfortunately, unlike mockingbirds, geckos don't get much practice in the air.

Whump! I landed heavily, thwacking my head on a pole. Stars danced before my eyes like talent night at the local YMCA. Through the stars, I saw the cobra's two-fanged smile.

"Ssso long, sssucker," he said. Jimmy King Cobra turned and began to slither through the boiler-room door.

But as he did, an eerie melody arose—a song of India, reeking of enchantment and moonlight. A real flute, played by a real snake charmer? I staggered to my feet and stepped closer.

The door swung open. Jimmy King Cobra swayed

to the rhythm of the melody coming from...
Natalie's beak?

Leave it to a mockingbird. She could have played
first flute in the school band—without an instru-
ment. Waving her beak to and fro, Natalie led the
mesmerized cobra back outside, away from the covered hallway and the boiler room.

My partner stepped backward onto the grass, the
snake following her obediently.

Shhoomp! A thick net sailed from the roof, land-
ing heavily on the cobra. It was followed closely by
Maureen DeBree, the crafty mongoose.

As Natalie continued her hypnotic song, the janitor rolled and tied and trussed the big snake like an
old garden hose. She used knots no Girl Scout ever
knew. And for a grand finale, she taped the cobra's
mouth shut, then hooked the roll on to her tool belt.

"Duct tape," she rasped. "Don't never leave
home without it."

20

All's Well That Ends

Natalie came to stand beside me. "Well, that's that," she said. "Case closed."

"Not quite," I said, grabbing her shoulder. "I heard another ghost that day. Jimmy's got a mate, and she's still on the loose."

Ms. DeBree's tail bristled. "Not for long. Come with me."

We trailed her into the boiler room, where two tall canisters stood like sentries. Following her lead, we put on gas masks and released the bottled gas into the heating system.

"What's the story?" I asked.

The mongoose's muffled voice came through the mask. "See, after you went and told me 'bout the ghosts in the vents, I put two and three together," she said. "That stinking mama cobra was building a nest in the heating ducts somewheres. This should flush 'er out."

Sure enough, we soon heard a scuttling in the wide pipes. It drew nearer, accompanied by what sounded like high-pitched giggles.

"Grab this," said Ms. DeBree. She handed us the ends of another rope net.

With an explosion of laughter, a hugely pregnant cobra burst from the heating duct like a streamer from a party favor, straight into our trap. As the mongoose tied up the second snake, I asked, "What kind of gas was that, anyway?"

"Laughing gas," she chuckled. "Eh, you know what they say: Let a smile be your umbrella—"

"And you'll get a mouthful of rain," I said.

We had one wacky janitor. But she sure got the job done.

The next day was one of my better ones at Emerson Hicky Elementary. True, I didn't get out of taking my history test. But overall, life was good.

Once he got past being mad at how open house had turned into a mass giggle-athon, Principal Zero canceled my lifelong detention and dish-washing duty. Minnie Stroney resigned in disgrace and took a job as a prison cook.

(We later found her secret plans for taking over

the cafeteria: She was going to serve nothing but Mystery Meat, Monday through Friday.)

The cobras, still wrapped up like toxic Christmas gifts, were thrown into the slammer. The cops gave the snakes a choice: undergo a long, painful operation to remove their poison sacs, or change their address permanently.

That morning's slow boat for Bombay had two extra passengers.

I'd like to say that on that happy Tuesday, Rocky Rhode and her fellow roughnecks changed their ways and became my bosom buddies. I'd like to say that, but Mom always told me not to lie.

Truth is, they stayed as rotten as ever. But at least Rocky took me off her "must kill now" list and put me on "kill waiting."

All these things warmed the cockles of my heart. But lunchtime brought the best news of all.

Natalie and I were standing in line. When we reached Mrs. Bagoong, she piled extra cockroach cupcakes onto our trays. Her smile beamed like a glowworm in a light socket.

"Well done, detectives," she said. The burly iguana reached into her apron pocket and handed me a big golden key. "Chet, this is for you."

I held it reverently in my hand. "The key to the lunchroom?"

Natalie poked her beak closer and sniffed. "Uh, Chet? Before you get too excited, you might want to unwrap it."

"Huh?"

I tapped the key. It wasn't metal. I peeled back the gold foil wrapping to find . . . chocolate! I grinned back at Mrs. Bagoong.

It might not have been the key to the lunchroom, but it was the key to this detective's heart.

And a case that ends with chocolate is a darn good case, in my book.

**Someone's turning students into zombies . . .
and Chet's got to find out who,
before *he* ends up sleeping "The Big Nap."**

I looked around. There he was, two seats up: Bo
Newt, your fourth-grade source for rubber-band guns,
fart cushions, art supplies, and whatever else would dis-
turb the peace.

I hissed at him, "Bo! Lend me your eraser."

Nothing. His eyes watched Mr. Ratnose. The back
of Bo's thick head gleamed slightly, like a fridge in the
moonlight.

Stronger measures were needed.

The spitwad sailed from my straw and bounced off
Bo Newt's head with a satisfying *thwop!*

"Duhhh." Bo turned to me with a loose grin. His eyes
were as empty as a bully's mailbox on Valentine's Day.

"I said, can I borrow your eraser?" I waved a hand
before his face. But my classmate kept on staring like his
choochoo didn't go back to the station anymore.

"Science good," he slurred.

Uh-oh.

Something was definitely wrong. I'd seen students
lobotomized by a boring science class before, but they
usually snapped out of it after you hit them with a spitwad or pulled on their tail.

"Bo, you okay?" I said.

He put a finger to his lips. "*Shhh*. Teacher talking."

I frowned. Since when had Bo Newt ever cared about how much lava could fit into a lava lamp?

A quiet snicker drifted over from the next row. The new kid, that skinny weasel from the playground, waggled his eyebrows at me and imitated Bo's blank face.

"He's as clueless as a porcupine at a polka lesson," Sammy whispered.

It was pretty rude. But I had to admit, I liked the way he put things. It reminded me of someone.

But I couldn't stop to think who. My detective instincts kicked in.

First, Eena Moe went weird. Now, something had turned Bo the Brat into Percival Priss, Good Student and All-around Zombie.

One zombie is normal. But two zombies is strange, even for Emerson Hicky.

I smelled a mystery. And where mystery led, I followed.

Especially if it led away from science class.

Look for more mysteries from the Tattered Casebook of Chet Gecko in hardcover and paperback

Case #1 *The Chameleon Wore Chartreuse*

Some cases start rough, some cases start easy. This one started with a dame. (That's what we private eyes call a girl.) She was cute and green and scaly. She looked like trouble and smelled like . . . grasshoppers.

Shirley Chameleon came to me when her little brother, Billy, turned up missing. (I suspect she also came to spread cooties, but that's another story.) She turned on the tears. She promised me some stinkbug pie. I said I'd find the brat.

But when his trail led to a certain stinky-breathed, bad-tempered, jumbo-size Gila monster, I thought I'd bitten off more than I could chew. Worse, I had to chew fast: If I didn't find Billy in time, it would be bye-bye, stinkbug pie.

Case #2 *The Mystery of Mr. Nice*

How would you know if some criminal mastermind tried to impersonate your principal? My first clue: He was nice to me.

This fiend tried everything—flattery, friendship, food—but he still couldn't keep me off the case. Natalie and I followed a trail of clues as thin as the cheese on a cafeteria hamburger. And we found a ring of corruption that went from the janitor right up to Mr. Big.

In the nick of time, we rescued Principal Zero and busted up the PTA meeting, putting a stop to the evil genius. And what thanks did we get? Just the usual. A cold handshake and a warm soda.

But that's all in a day's work for a private eye.

Case #5   *The Hamster of the Baskervilles*

Elementary school is a wild place. But this was ridiculous.

Someone—or some*thing*—was tearing up Emerson Hicky. Classrooms were trashed. Walls were gnawed. Mysterious tunnels riddled the playground like worm chunks in a pan of earthworm lasagna.

But nobody could spot the culprit, let alone catch him.

I don't believe in the supernatural. My idea of voodoo is my mom's cockroach-ripple ice cream.

Then, a teacher reported seeing a monster on full-moon night, and I got the call.

At the end of a twisted trail of clues, I had to answer the burning question: Was it a vicious, supernatural were-hamster on the loose, or just another science-fair project gone wrong?

Case #6 *This Gum for Hire*

Never thought I'd see the day when one of my worst enemies would hire me for a case. Herman the Gila Monster was a sixth-grade hoodlum with a first-rate left hook. He told me someone was disappearing the football team, and he had to put a stop to it. *Big whoop.*

He told me he was being blamed for the kidnappings, and he had to clear his name. *Boo hoo.*

Then, he said that I could either take the case and earn a nice reward, or have my face rearranged like a bargain-basement Picasso painted by a spastic chimp.

I took the case.

But before I could find the kidnapper, I had to go undercover. And that meant facing something that scared me worse than a chorus line of criminals in steel-toed boots: P.E. class.

	DATE DUE		